# Percy

Based on
**The Railway Series**
by the
**Rev. W. Awdry**

Illustrations by
**Robin Davies and
Creative Design**

**EGMONT**

# EGMONT

*We bring stories to life*

First published in Great Britain in 2016
by Egmont UK Limited
The Yellow Building, 1 Nicholas Road, London W11 4AN

Thomas the Tank Engine & Friends™

CREATED BY BRITT ALLCROFT

HiT entertainment

ISBN 978 1 4052 7981 9
62427/1
Printed in Italy

Stay safe online. Egmont is not responsible for content hosted by third parties.

Written by Emily Stead. Designed by Martin Aggett.

FSC
MIX
Paper
FSC® C018306

Egmont is passionate about helping to preserve the world's remaining ancient forests.
We only use paper from legal and sustainable forest sources.

This book is made from paper certified by the Forest Stewardship Council® (FSC®),
an organisation dedicated to promoting responsible management of forest resources.
For more information on the FSC, please visit www.fsc.org. To learn more about Egmont's
sustainable paper policy, please visit www.egmont.co.uk/ethical

*This story is about my good
friend Percy, the Number 6 engine.
He's small but he's not afraid to play tricks
on the bigger engines. Here's how
he became a Really Useful Engine
and stopped his silly tricks . . .*

There was once a tank engine called Percy, who was small and green and loved to play tricks.

**"Peep! Peep!** Hurry up, Gordon!" Percy whistled one day. "Your Express train is ready!"

But when Gordon steamed out of the Shed, all that was waiting for him was a train of dirty coal trucks! Gordon was very cross.

Percy played a trick on James next. "Wait here, James," said Percy. "The Fat Controller is coming with a **special train** for you."

James stayed in his Shed all morning, but The Fat Controller never came! The other engines had to do all James' work.

When The Fat Controller found out about Percy's trick, the little engine was in **big trouble**.

"Useful Engines do not waste time playing silly tricks!" The Fat Controller shouted.

The next day, Percy had to collect some children from the beach. He borrowed Thomas' carriages, Annie and Clarabel.

Percy **steamed** to the station as a big storm began to break. He wished he were back in his nice warm Shed!

**"Hurry! Hurry!"** Percy told his passengers. He shivered from funnel to footplate as the thunder crashed all around.

Percy knew that he needed to be a **Really Useful Engine** and get the children home safely.

Raindrops bounced off his boiler as Percy puffed **bravely** down the track.

Suddenly, Percy found himself wheel-deep in water. The river had burst its banks!

"We must keep going, we must keep going," sang Annie and Clarabel.

But before long Percy's Driver had to stop the train. Percy's fire had almost gone out! He needed more fuel, but there wasn't any more coal.

"We'll have to pull up the floorboards and burn the wood," said Percy's Fireman.

With his fire burning brightly again, Percy felt much better.

Suddenly there was a **Buzz! Buzz!** in the sky.

It was Harold the Helicopter. He dropped a parcel, which landed with a **BUMP!**

Inside were sandwiches and hot chocolate for the passengers and crew!

**"Peep! Peep!** Thank you, Harold!" Percy whistled, as he pushed on through the flood.

Percy was losing steam, but he kept on going and with a great **whoosh** of steam he pulled clear of the flood.

"Well done, Percy!" The Fat Controller smiled, as Percy puffed into the station. "What a **Really Useful Engine** you are!"

"**Pip! Peep!** Thank you, Sir!" said Percy, feeling very proud.

The tale of how Percy had saved his passengers from the storm soon reached the Shed.

Gordon and James weren't cross with Percy anymore. "You're very brave . . . for a little engine!" said Gordon kindly.

Now that Percy knew how to be a **Really Useful Engine,** he soon forgot all about playing tricks!

# More about Percy

coal bunker

whistle

boiler

dome

funnel

brake-pipe hose

cab door

6

coupling hook

footplate

connecting rod

cylinders

buffer

# Percy's challenge to you

Look back through the pages of this book
and see if you can spot:

rainbow

swan

poster of James

phone box

signal

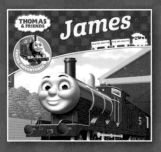
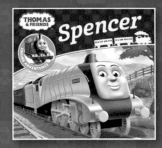
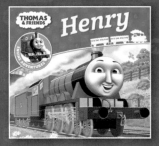
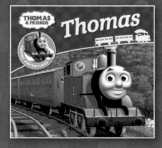